W9-BAY-986

No Need for Monty

by JAMES STEVENSON

Greenwillow Books New York

FIRST EDITION   10 9 8 7 6 5 4 3 2 1

BLACK PEN-LINE AND WATERCOLOR PAINTS WERE USED
TO PREPARE THE FULL-COLOR ART.

LIBRARY OF CONGRESS CATALOGING-IN-PUBLICATION DATA
STEVENSON, JAMES, (DATE)
NO NEED FOR MONTY.
SUMMARY: CONVINCED THAT CROSSING THE RIVER ON THE BACK
OF MONTY THE ALLIGATOR IS TOO SLOW, THE ANIMALS TRY TO
FIND A FASTER WAY TO GET THEIR CHILDREN TO SCHOOL.
[1. ALLIGATORS—FICTION.   2. ANIMALS—FICTION]   I. TITLE.
PZ7.S84748NOK 1987   [E]   86-22818
ISBN 0-688-07083-3   ISBN 0-688-07084-1 (LIB. BDG.)

To Luca

EVERY MORNING, MONTY GAVE DORIS AND ARTHUR AND TOM A RIDE ACROSS THE RIVER TO SCHOOL.

EVERY AFTERNOON, MONTY GAVE THEM A RIDE HOME AGAIN.

IT DIDN'T MATTER WHAT THE WEATHER WAS...

MONTY ALWAYS CAME.

ONE DAY, SOME OF THE GROWN-UPS
WERE STANDING BY THE RIVER...

ARE YOU TIRED?
DO YOU WANT ME TO HELP ROW?
NO! LEAVE ME ALONE!
I GUESS THEY DIDN'T SEE US...
MAYBE WE'RE GOING TOO FAST...

CAN'T YOU ROW A BIT FASTER, KIRKHAM?
NO!
WE'RE NOT MOVING AT ALL... LOOKS LIKE WE'RE IN THE MUD...
GLUP

HOLD TIGHT! YOU'LL BE ACROSS THE RIVER IN HALF THE SPEED OF AN ALLIGATOR!
OH, BOY!
SOME FUN!
SKEEK!

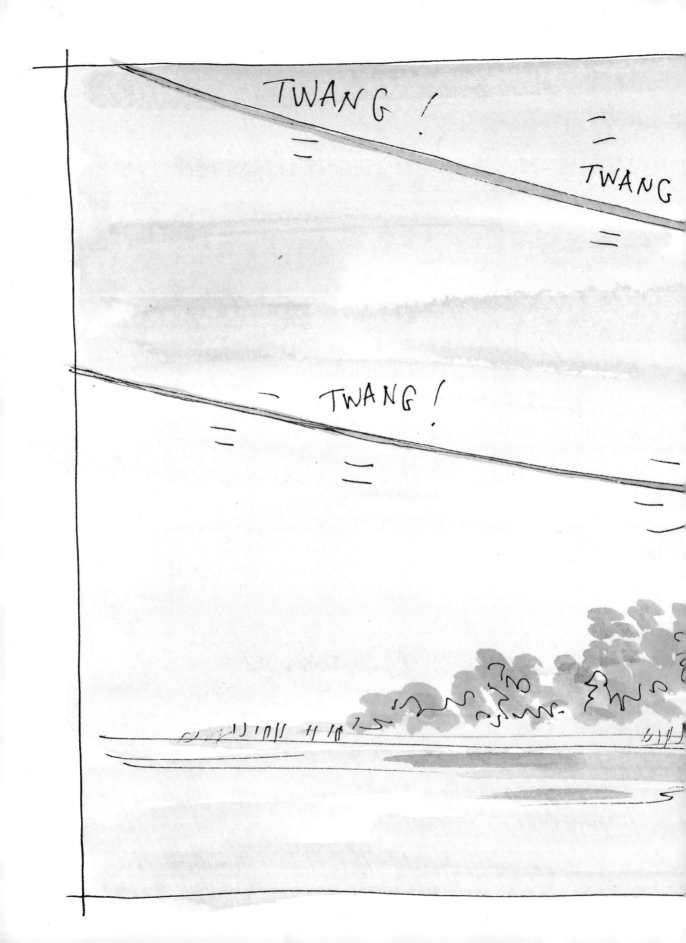

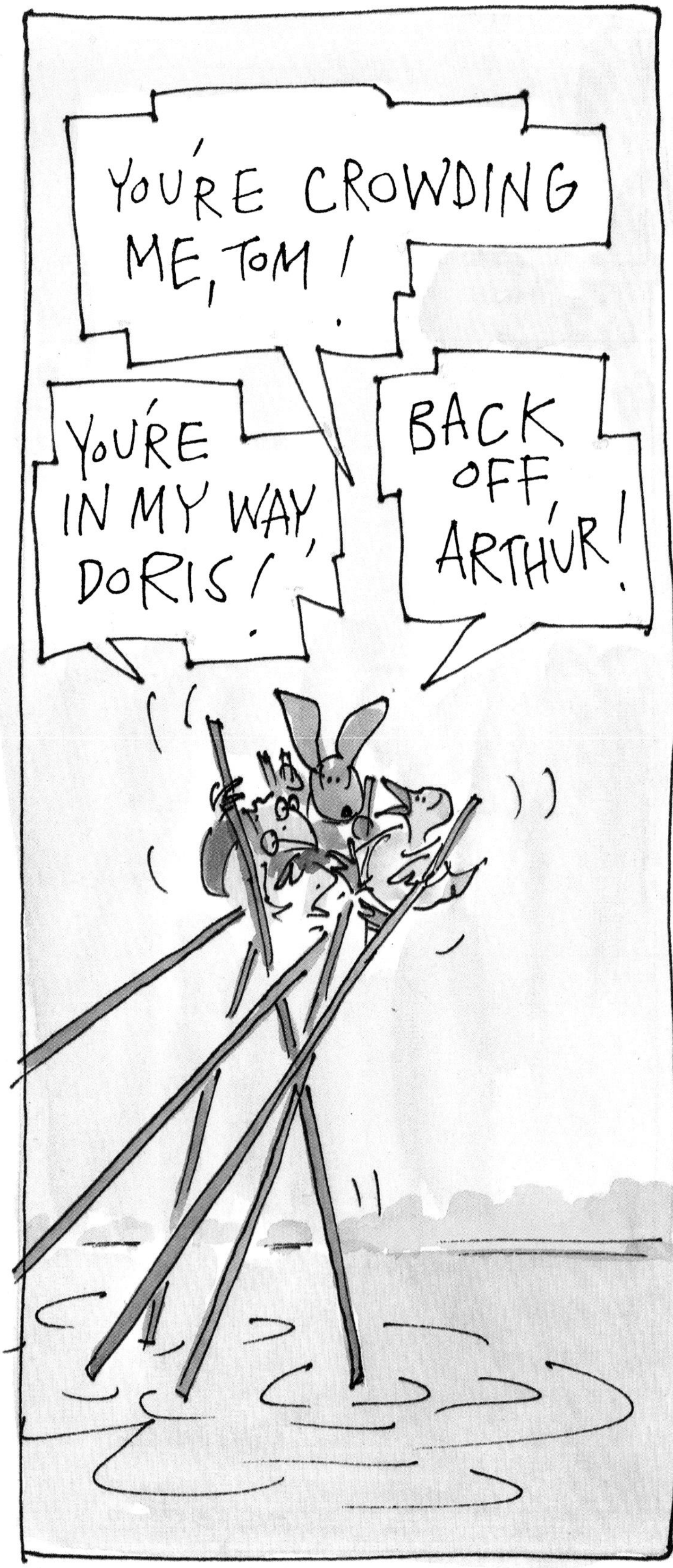
YOU'RE CROWDING ME, TOM!
YOU'RE IN MY WAY, DORIS!
BACK OFF, ARTHUR!

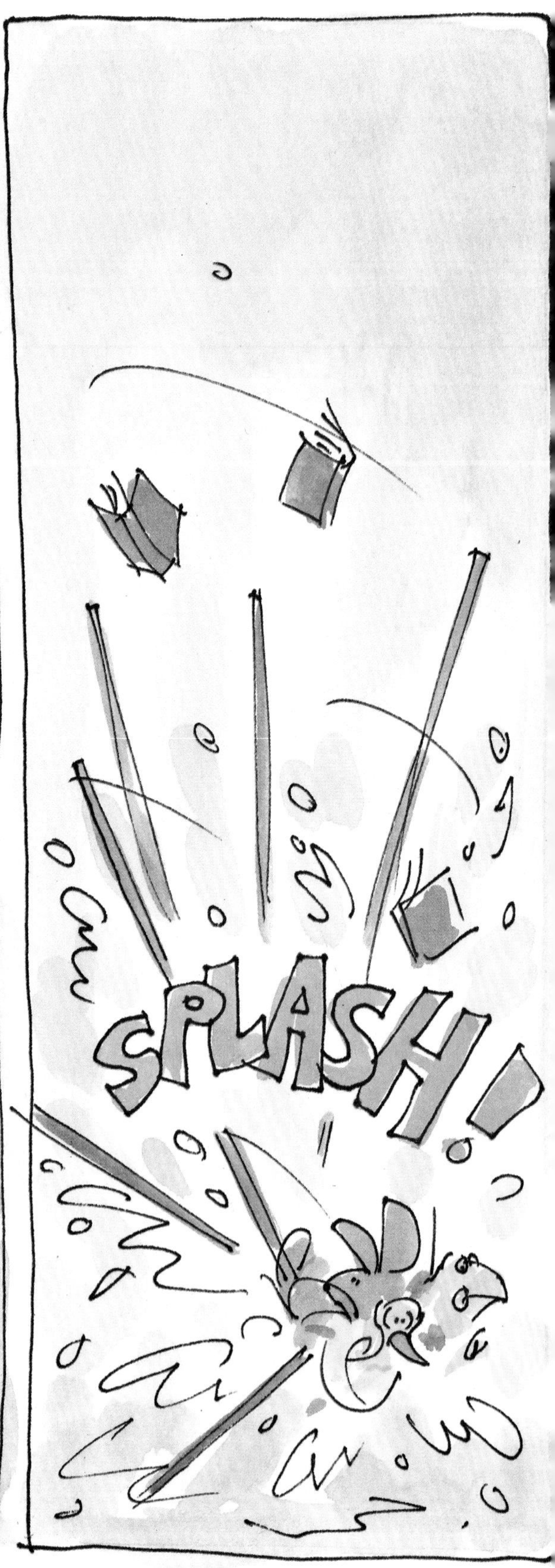
SPLASH!